Fuego

J. R. ORTIZ

FUEGO is a fictional play/narrative/novel/book of poetry.

Any resemblance of characters in the play/narrative/novel/book of poetry to real persons, living or dead, is purely coincidental and not intentional.

ISBN: 0692799176
ISBN 13: 9780692799178
Library of Congress Control Number: 2016917828
AMERICAN AMARANTH LLC, Miami, FL

THIS STORY IS DEDICATED TO ALL THOSE WITH FREEDOM IN THEIR SPIRITS AND LIGHT IN THEIR HEARTS, AND THE WILL AND SACRIFICE TO SEE IT THROUGH...

Table of Contents

Prologue

FUEGO is the fictional story of Jorge Sierra, a Cuban poet and painter during the times of Fidel Castro's revolution. Also an opponent of Fulgencio Batista's corrupt prior regime, he refuses to accept the betrayals of the Cuban Revolution. With a loving family, wife, and child, the freedom fighter drops the pen and brush and takes up the gun in struggle against communist tyranny in his island home. Taken prisoner after the failed Bay of Pigs invasion, Sierra goes to the infamous prison, La Cabaña, in Havana. FUEGO depicts the final twenty-four hours in a patriot's life.

SunKissed

In school study room across the way,
by blue picture window and sunlit bay,
sat a girl of special fantasy and golden dreams,
with dark hair and eyes, and face most supremes...

I gazed in open wonder at magic form,
as she read a book in bright morning light.
Lost in sunbeams and beauty silent storm,
my mind entranced in sun-kissed flight...

Glancing slow at me, she caught my stare.
Smiled and winked, and laid me bare.
I walked over and pulled a chair,
and the girl accepted bold and clear dare...

Admitting with teen spirit, equal interest and delight,
she pulled me closer without a fight.
Magnificent splendor of youthful energy,
the source of all the world's love poetry...

Joy of Your Hand

Give me your hand…
In hourglass, slow grains of beach sand…
Mystic silence, but in ear great music band…
Temptation of flesh can barely withstand…

Delicate fine fingers like snake trails,
along love paths by sea and lake shore.
Tiny boats bob on waters with bright color sails,
blues and pinks, and some with dark wood oar.

I gaze and wonder of lure,
of body so composite and pure.
Splendid bone and pulp and skin,
so alluring and bringing of original sin.

Mound and gorge of breast and rear,
so too arms and shoulders and thighs.
Holy clam temple manhood to smear,
all for me to tantalize and carnalize.

Festival of thought and desire,
as I lay beside you on fire.
So much to admire and acquire.
What must I do to supply her?

Grand epic ecstasy and pleasure,
life together real final treasure...
Nature so simple, so divine,
all I truly need is joy of hand in mine...

Impressions of a Day

On this day, day of all days...
Morning dawn bloomed in all color.
Golden sunrise kissed violet purple horizon.
Rays of soft yellow light blanched stars to sleep.
Dark blue sky eased to cobalt white.
Sea awakened in aquamarine foam.
Earth winds spun us to a stop,
hand in hand...

On this day, day of all days...
Destiny was born, you and I.
Rainbows filled, and butterflies were free.
Music was true and never faded.
Desires ever lasted.
Mystic universe, infinite space and time,
ether of life demanded we be one.
One heart, one soul...

On this day, day of all days...
Love was confirmed.
Joy sprung more joyous,
hope more hopeful,
faith more deep...

On this day, day of all days...
You and I – WE – became forever,
to soothe and support,
to nourish and devour,
to share and grow,
for all of time...

Beware the Rebel Mask

Behind confusing masks and masquerade,
screams for revolutionary justice and change laid.
Beneath dirty beards and long hair crusade,
holding rifle, hand grenade, and knife blade,
exist only sad history of peoples betrayed...

With hidden intent to control and oppress,
never to consider fair idea, but to suppress,
robbing and stealing all you possess,
to trial and death without due process.
All in putrid stench of purulent abscess...

Why men with such evil design?
With low-life creature pathos to sicken and malign.
Devils from hell – pathetic, tragic, and asinine.
We need more soldiers of valor and honor to outshine.
Those with truth and courage in hearts genuine...

Temperature of Color

Disc of sun over Varadero in morning,
surf azure and sky apricot…
Bands of back-lit tangerine and lemon sunset,
lavender and vivid violet over a coral sanguine sea…

Cinnamon soil and verdant Viñales and Yumurí,
with stone hills and countless Royal Palms in misty dawn…

Turquoise waters at mid-day,
sliding over light-drenched pale sand beaches…

Pastels and earth tones of Trinidad and Cienfuegos,
and wet hues of Zapata…

Living shades of flora and fauna,
breathing and praising homeland…

Polymita swirls of vibrant orange,
yellow, cherry, and baby blue…

Iridescent emerald ZunZún,
bright greens and pinks of the Tody…

Red clouds of twilight,
morning star white and cerulean Tocororo…

The radiant warm colors of Cuba,
vital and dynamic in spirit...
Like her people...

Tears in Oil

I have painted Cuba with tears in oil...
Much salt of the earth in my images.

How can a land have grand passion, faith, and love,
and also so many shortcomings and failings?

High art and science,
joy of life,
determination and character,
and also great ineptitude to govern herself,
fairly and peacefully.

Where is the human balance for survivability and
achievement,
and advancement into the future?

Where are the thoughtful minds,
so required of her culture?

We can no longer have false and wasted sacrifice.
We need true prophets,
true leaders,
true Cubans...

The Human Trace

I brush across the canvas - the human trace...
In thick paint and color, I show the condition of Man.
Toils and struggles,
deprivations...

In dark and light,
in clear and imagined,
in figure and abstract,
I depict life's challenges...

Yet too, and always stronger,
I reflect on gentle angels.
The joys, wishes, and aspirations.
The love...

It is the mixture of all between birth and death,
the sound and fury,
the rise and fall,
the good and evil,
that I describe in the human trace.

Dear Beloved

No deep sea trek, desert walk, or mountain climb,
no cross of vast forest green or grim jungle scare,
nor slow descent or dismal crash of falling time,
no obstacles – real of mind – impair or despair…

Sound and strong of body or not,
muscle and sinew struggle for want,
with or without clear sense of thought,
no fear, no hear of chance to daunt…

No tight funnel wind or rain of storm,
nor angry celestial show of electric light,
no thunder or force of bolt sky high swarm,
or lack of open sight in a coal black night…

In horrid famine, flood or drought,
pestilence and plague, anarchy and war,
I regardless of cause or reason am devout,
to fight and fight for you – if not, what for?

Inside deep, deep inside my central soul's core,
I feel you living and loving more and more, and more.
If despite all try, I'm kept from you in body form -
Dear Beloved – in my heart you'll remain forever warm…

ACT I

First Hours

There was passion fire in me for all things right and fine – science and theory, art, and love --- Love and desire of wife and child, country, the just world…

There was also fire raging against all things unjust and un-fine. I could not accept the many wrongs I saw evolving in my land – the country of my birth… Conviction had urged me on, forcing my hand to drop the brush and pen, and pick up the gun…

I pressed my face hard against the rusted ancient iron bars to catch the late spring dawn tropical mist rain. With eyes closed, the fresh water washed into my parched mouth and down my throat like smooth aged Cuban rum. At once, I could sense the rush of every river in every valley of Cuba. I could see in my mind's eye every white ocean wave break on every white sand beach, every green hillside in twilight, every palm swing in the breezes. I could smell every cigar and cup of rich coffee...

The sun was beginning to rise above an ocean purple horizon. I could feel the beams of light on my skin, warming me from the inside out. It would be another day with mixed blue, white, and gray in the sky - with columns of rain in patches pouring over Havana. The sun always peeking through its light and producing the many natural rainbow colors I adored so much to paint.

I had admired Cuba's natural light since my rural youth. It was uniquely brilliant even on a cloudy day. In summer as a boy, I'd awaken before earliest light and wait for the sunrise. I'd then launch myself across the valley near our Trinidad ranch under the golden dome, running through dense stands of Royal Palm and groves of coffee plants, past a cool flowing river from the upper mountain reaches, and into rich fields of fruit and vegetables. Violet hillsides would go blue, then verdant green, with the warm drench of photonic waves. In the Escambray mountains, sunlight would fall on the hardwood forests with tall canopies like sacred light on a church altar. Beams would filter through the high leaves and drop on me like honey from heaven. Nature would come alive with color, clean fresh air, and the sound of rushing waters...

I finally opened my eyes. I looked through the bars of my prison cell at La Cabaña, and saw the light I loved so much begin to fall on Old Havana and our capitol building. I was greatly saddened by my fate, and my country's fate. How had Cuba fallen into so much disrepair? --- I wondered for the millionth time.

Human activity was building along the seaside Malecón. The Cuban people were trying their best to return to a "normal" life after our failed Bay of Pigs invasion.

As a CIA operative, I had infiltrated into Cuba before the invasion to provide intelligence on government troop movements near the beachhead, blow bridges, and prevent militia soldiers from reaching Playa Girón. On the morning of the invasion, our eight-man team was overwhelmed by a large force of Castro soldiers. I and two other survivors, whom I never saw again, were taken prisoner. Arriving at La Cabaña the next day, I was thrown into a special cell overlooking Havana – so that I could see all of her all the time, day and night, and know I'd never walk or paint her streets again.

With me in prison was a young boy, no older than 19 or 20, captured on the invasion beaches. He was in terrible condition, with one of his legs torn up by machine gun fire. I had cared for him over the past four weeks. I too had a ragged wound in my leg which refused to heal.

"How are you feeling, Boy?" I asked, turning from Havana.

"Mierda," he answered in weak voice, sitting with his back against cold mossy limestone.

"Where am I?"

"We're in La Cabaña prison, so it's alright to feel like shit," I said. "You've been in and out of consciousness for the past month, fevering up with an infected wound in your leg. With a little help from our guard, I've been able to get you better," I gestured toward the guard peering through the small barred hole in the cell door, before he moved away.

"What's your name, Boy?" I asked to refresh his memory again, as I had done many times before.

"Victor Perez," he said.

"Who are you to merit the best cage in this prison, the only one to have a full view of the city and sea?" I grinned.

"I don't know if I'm anyone special," muttered the boy, "but my father was the head of the philosophy department at the University of Havana -- Dr. Jaime Perez. He was a vocal critic of Castro after the revolution and paid with his life."

"Yes... I know of him. He was also critical of Batista before the war. He was executed in this prison, in the months after Castro taking power... I remember his story well."

"And you?" Inquired the boy.

"Jorge Sierra is my name. And I too was an adversary of Batista, and of Castro after his betrayal."

"Jorge Sierra, the famous poet and painter?"

"Poet and painter, yes...

"Famous?

"It's not for me to say..."

"But your father was governor of Las Villas under Batista," stated the boy, not understanding.

"Yes he was... I love my father, but I never loved Batista," I smiled...

Victor was physically exhausted from his many days battling infection and mental confusion. I often tried to stimulate his memories, hoping his energies would follow.

"Here, Boy... Take some water and bread," I urged. "The guard will bring some soup later."

"Why is the guard helping us?" Questioned the boy.

"It's a complicated and long story, Boy... It doesn't matter at this point. Just eat and drink as much as possible. Let's stay strong and hope for an American invasion soon."

I moved over to the opposite wall and continued my work, scratching heavily into the ancient coral stone with a broken spoon. I was nearly finished with my intent. It had taken form like I had hoped. Victor slowly ate a moldy hard piece of bread.

"A few years ago, with my parents, I saw an exhibition of your paintings at the university. They were fond of your work, Jorge."

"Did you enjoy the show?" I asked.

"Most certainly... Especially the abstract flowers... I was somewhat ashamed, I remember, liking flowers – being nearly a man."

"There's nothing unmanly about enjoying the beauty of flowers," I stated with emphasis... "Besides, my flowers were abstractions of female genitalia, and their precious beauty," I laughed slightly.

"Did you study poetry and art at the university, Jorge?"

"No, Boy... I studied electrical engineering... But I wasn't much of an engineer... I preferred to write and paint... In retrospect, I suppose the mathematics and physics, and the arts, fed off each other... Objective measurements and the soul searches...

"Understanding life --- estimating positions of electrons spinning around the nucleus of an atom, or of planets around a star sun; calculating the expansion speed of the universe; measuring momentum or inertia of a moving object, or the tensile strength of a material; the conduction of heat in a metal; or the concentrations of gases in human blood; the speed of action potentials along the axon of a human nerve cell; knowing the facts of our solar system, or the evolution of Man...

"You may be able to answer many questions of physical existence with science... But never, absolutely never, will you understand depths of love or the angst of betrayal and loss, or the beauty of color of sea and sky and flower, with mathematics or physics...

"I truly believe understanding life requires a soul, and the mindful urge to explore and test that soul..."

The boy seemed interested in what I had to say.

"What did you enjoy more, writing poetry or painting?"

I continued to work on the wall with my back to the boy. There wasn't much time, I thought.

"I painted for the eyes, and wrote prose for the ears... Between those senses lay the mind and soul... I enjoyed connecting with people's deepest thoughts, their hopes and dreams... My pen and brush were tools to achieve my artistic desired effects.

"I enjoyed a poem and a picture equally, because both could move you equally.

"To appreciate the arts, Boy, one must immerse into the inner workings of the creative design... You must throw yourself into the fire of the poem or painting, and be willing to get burned by it," I said strongly, turning from the wall.

"I've read many of your poems, Jorge... But I'm not familiar with the paintings, other than the lady flowers. My father once mentioned you had passed through several phases of works. He felt all were inspirational and beautiful, especially your depictions of the Cuban woman."

"As an adolescent in the late 40s, I painted mainly classic rural Cuban landscapes. The landscapes became quickly abstract; and as a university student, I began several years of abstract expressionistic figuration of women. With the injustices of the revolution, I turned to counter-revolutionary modern expressions. My last series of firing squad executions got the attention of many people, including Fidel.

"I've learned through the years that to write poetry and paint – you must love... Even when you paint things and people you hate, you must love something deeply in order to hate something else enough to permanently render it into the black abyss of history.

"We all have prejudices, Boy... Mine are injustice and ignorance... They overtook whatever little talent I had. My attempts to express our reality have not been helpful for Cuba or myself. I don't believe I've been consequential in the struggle to liberate our country. Stringing together pretty words, or painting a pretty picture is not enough. Man has been killing Man too long to allow sentiment in the way."

"You're wrong, Jorge!" said the boy with raised voice, sitting next to me. "Words and pictures, like a special woman, can launch a thousand ships or field an army of a million men. That's what they're afraid of, Jorge... The power to move hearts..."

"Do you have a girl, Victor?" I asked in hushed tone.

"Yes... Jacqueline... We were students together at the university. She's the finest girl I've ever known, with the prettiest face and legs in Cuba. She has a heart of gold, and sings like a songbird too."

"Do you love her?" I inquired in a whisper.

The boy slowly nodded, his eyes watering like wet grapes.

Staring at the wall, I returned to my work with my broken fingers and spoon.

"Do you have children, Jorge?" Questioned Victor in a tender voice.

"A little girl named Olivia," I answered, without looking back at him.

"How old is she?"

"Too young," I murmured...

"And your woman?" The boy asked.

"Yes... I too love a woman," I whispered, continuing my work.

"Did you ever paint her?" He asked.

"She was in all my works, all the poems and paintings beyond the early landscapes... My depictions of the Cuban countryside were only waiting for her inspiration to enter them."

I pressed hard with the spoon into the old limestone blocks. Shattered pieces of coral fell at my bare feet. Blood from my fingers flowed into the porous rock, leaving crimson and wine colored stone trails.

"Are you familiar with the ancient East Asian philosophy of the 'Red String of Fate'?" I asked, now turning again to face the boy.

The young man nodded no, now laying on the cold dirty floor.

"It's a force mystically connecting destined lovers, regardless of time or conditions... It never breaks, and never releases from your hearts.

"One cool spring morning, a few years ago, I studied in a café by the sea. I was preparing for an important engineering oral examination... Across at short distance, a large open picture window allowed the ocean breezes to settle on me. The sky and sea were a brilliant blue, and the horizon was nearly invisible from the blending of color. Golden yellow light in a radiant cone lit the room... I was so taken by the natural beauty and the smell of the sea, that I pulled a sketch pad from my bag and began re-creating the image... Almost finished, a young woman out of nowhere sat at the table by the window... She was stunning, with the most angelic face I'd ever seen. Her dark hair and eyes contrasted gently with her white smooth skin... She opened a book and began to read... I caringly drew her into my picture, falling in love with every dot and line defined. I couldn't help but stare as I worked to get her every detail... Sunbeams swirled around her like yellow fire in an aura. The sea and sky blue settled like sapphire in background on a magic canvas... She looked up and saw me gazing. She winked and smiled, inviting me to share closer. I happily obliged. As I sat beside her with her image in my hand, I realized she was reading a book of my love poetry... I succumbed to the 'Red String'. In no time, my lady had become reason for my birth."

"So your art was this woman," said the boy.

"No... My art is this woman..."

The young man and I were not far apart in age, or in love of country, or in love of a woman. We both wished with all our hearts to be free, to share our lives with our girls and people. We both had joy in our spirits and desire to live. Somehow, I – a painter and poet, and Victor – a university student son of a philosophy professor, had been wrapped up in a human calamity, a crazy revolution and national shift to tyranny. We were enemies of the new communist state, enemies of Fidel...

A loud volley of gunshot sounded outside. It echoed into our cell, filling our little space with dread and sadness.

I limped back to the barred window facing Havana and the sea, and waited for the next pistol shot to the head. It came quickly, and another patriot was dead.

Soft rain fell again on my face and mixed with tears for the fallen, the executed of the oppressive state. The murders would last all day, just like yesterday and the days before. "Enemies" of the new Cuba would be eliminated like rabid dogs in the street. The "people" demanded it, screamed Fidel Castro. The new Cubans would need to be "compliant" with the orderly state. They would be all children of the revolution.

"Executions?" The boy somberly questioned.

"Sacrifices for Fidel's revolution," I answered, squeezing tightly the iron bars caging me.

"Most are just young boys, unwilling and unable to be ruled by crazy power-hungry narcissists. They'd rather fight for freedom and die, than live as slaves of crazy ideology and mad men... There will be many more this morning, like all mornings... The sun has risen, and it will shine God's light on the sick doings here," I said angrily.

The same tropical light of the sun which had illuminated my art and life, now shed its fire on wrong-doings in my land. Evil ways would be seen and recorded in the hearts of men, and never forgotten. God's justice would come one day.

I stayed by the window for at least an hour, as I usually did every morning. The fusillades repeated as they usually did, ending the lives of many. The cries for freedom from the condemned before riflemen, and the liberty shouts from jailed listeners of history, repeated as they usually did. In the great sorrows, many tears were dropped for friends and family.

I looked up into the sky at a passing cloud. White and feathery like cotton, with wisps of gray mixed in, it flowed slowly beyond the city into the interior. I figured it would pass over towns and villages and people I had painted. Over rivers and waterfalls and beaches I had frequented. I wished to have floated on it, into freedom and another chance at life.

"Will we die in a salvo like the others, Jorge?" Asked the boy with worried tongue.

"All those with voices in this putrid fortress hell, Boy, will die... Your father was murdered for his opinions on the natural rights of Man. You fought for the same. All of us prisoners, with loud and strong voices against oppression, will die in fiery discharges from these brainwashed blood-thirsty animals!" I said angrily.

"Could they be willing to stamp out a voice like yours, so beloved by our people?" Doubted the boy. "Your expressions have been so important for all of us, Jorge. Your art symbolizes our culture."

"If my voice, as you say Victor, has been louder and stronger than most --- then, more likely, I will have a louder and stronger death than most," I murmured, listening to another pistol shot to the head of a patriot.

"I wonder what it feels to die?" Anguished the boy.

I stepped back from the window and returned to Victor's side on the cold limestone floor. He had suffered in violent fevers for several days, and had forgotten our many earlier talks into the night. The sepsis spells had weakened his memory and physical strength. He was only a shell of the bright smiled boy I had met a month earlier. Even wounded and unable to walk, his spirit had been tough and humane. I had noted a light in his heart, a joyous light of a boy with much to live for --- with hope unconsumed by worry or doubt. I had felt with all my soul, Victor was an emblematic Cuban boy. He had great love inside of him; and it had not been spoiled by the horrors around us... Earlier in our struggle, we had spoken many times of death...

"Perhaps it feels calmer than to be born," I answered tenderly. "Certainly calmer than to live..."

"I didn't much feel the machine gun fire to my leg, Jorge... Maybe to my chest won't hurt either," he hoped.

"Don't think about it so much, Victor. Close your eyes and dream about Jacqueline. Think of kissing her and holding her hand," I urged in hope also.

"Maybe the Americans will come," he tiredly whispered… "They wouldn't allow a Soviet satellite state so close to home… Would they, Jorge?"

"I think we must fend for ourselves, Boy," I said sadly. "They passed on a great opportunity at Playa Girón. Kennedy had a lapse in judgement which will cost America dearly. Leaders are sometimes caught in webs of mistakes which don't allow for easy resolution. Stuck in their own tight strictures, they miss chances for redemption, believing a saving counter-strike would highlight their original calamitous error. Only the Cuban people can save Cuba. They must decide whether they wish tyranny or a fresh start in freedom. The destiny of our nation lies in our hands and none other."

Many more rifle discharges filled the cool morning air. Castro and Guevara would continue their rage of revenge and control. For many more days and months and years, trucks of the executed bodies would be rolling out from the prison to mass graves close by.

"How does this happen?" Asked the boy.

"Being free does not come cheap, Victor… Liberty must be nurtured and respected. It can't be taken for granted. Like one loves a mother, a wife, a child, one must love freedom. Living free requires work. The body, mind, and soul must be invested. If not, they will be stolen away by nefarious characters who are more interested in ruling and enriching themselves than developing humane and productive societies. One cannot have advanced culture under the yoke of oppression. Cuba is learning this lesson again."

The small pass window on the cell door opened. The guard peeked through and quietly asked to see me. I went and put my face up close to him.

"Are you finished with your work?" He asked.

"Almost," I answered him.

"You must quicken your pace, Chiquillo. I've been informed your tribunal is today, in just a few hours. Guevara himself will preside. He has a thing for you, I was told. He took possession of some of your works from your mountain studio in the Escambray, some books of poetry and a painting. I was told the big canvas is red like blood, as his communist sympathies. They say he respects your work, but despises your spirit and symbol.

"I have arranged for your escape, Chiquillo Jorge. It's a dangerous plan, but with faith and luck I can get you out…"

"And the boy?" I asked.

"Impossible," said the guard, Samuel Velázquez… "It's not possible to get him out. I'm risking my life for you, Chiquillo, but for no one else."

"But you have helped me save his life so far, Samuel."

"There is a limit to what I can do, Chiquillo… I also must live for my wife and children."

"I can't leave without the boy," I whispered…

"Think hard about it, Jorge… This will be your only chance to see your wife and Olivia… To live, Chiquillo…"

"There's no more thinking, Samuel… It's me and the boy together…"

"Well… try to finish the work quickly, and let me see what I can do… Here is some soup for both of you. It's not much, but it'll keep you alive for now…"

I brought back a small tin of clear salty broth, made with meaty scraps and onions. I sat again with Victor.

"Why is the guard helping us, Jorge?"

"It's a long story, Boy... It's safer for you and him if we don't speak about it," I said.

"But I must know what he's done for me," demanded the boy.

"His food and water, and antibiotic powder have helped keep you alive... But the reasons why must remain secret," I stated.

"A man would not do this, endangering his life for an enemy, unless there were strong bonds, Jorge."

I shared the soup with the boy, and attempted to divert his thoughts. He persisted to inquire.

A cockroach scurried next to me. I slammed my hand on it, and placed the brown and yellow remains into the tin.

"More protein," I grinned. "Not even the cockroaches in Cuba are free."

"You have the hand of a dictator," laughed the boy.

"Each of us Cubans, Victor, have a little dictator inside."

The boy and I shared our meager lunch together, and tried our best to think of better times. The life of Samuel Velázquez kept eating at me like an unfinished canvas.

"Let me tell you a short story, Boy," I said softly...

The May rain outside had passed. The sky had cleared to light blue with a scattering of low-hanging white puffy clouds. The Caribbean Sea had a vibrant and crystal aqua color. In the natural beauty of Havana's paradise, firing squads continued the salvos of death...

"As a young boy, I lived on a large farm in rural Las Villas province near Trinidad. My father, a chemical engineer educated at MIT in Boston, had become prosperous in the sugar industry. He often traveled and was rarely home. My mother, older sisters and I managed the chores of the ranch, with assistance from several local campesinos. I learned to raise chickens and milk cows, and plant crops. I learned about animal diseases, vegetable-damaging insects, and climate effects on our harvest.

"Early on, I began to draw and paint the scenery around me. Whether under sun or moon, I enjoyed recreating the imagery - the beauty of Cuba's nature.

"A worker on the farm, a man in his thirties, would often take me into town to purchase oil pencils and paints, drawing paper and canvas. His wife and teen-aged son also worked and lived with us. Over time, his family became part of mine. He taught me to ride a horse, shoot a hunting rifle, throw a baseball. He would accompany me on my treks through the mountains to find those unique places I loved to paint, the waterfalls and flower filled valleys. He taught me old Cuban ballads, and how to play the guitar --- and also about girls and how to enamor them. I grew to love him like a father.

"When I was 13 or 14, on a cool winter Sunday morning, the man's wife and son used our family truck to go into Trinidad. On the main road, a drunken driver hit them head-on, killing them both.

"I remember the man's cries in his room that night, as my father prepared him for the funeral. I sat outside, under a clear moonless black sky. Every star twinkled bright to my eyes. I truly felt great pain for him and his loss. I cried also, and prayed for the souls of his wife and son.

"A few short months later, the man decided to leave our farm and try to start a new life in Oriente. The night before his departure, I worked without sleep to complete a painting of their family sitting on a mountain top facing the sea. I presented it to him with great sorrow in my heart the next morning. He greatly appreciated the gift, embraced me tightly, and bid his farewell.

"Years later, I learned he had remarried and started a new family. I never saw him again – until four weeks ago.

"Samuel Velázquez, the man who helped raise me, is our prison guard. Over the past days, he has provided us with nutrition and antibiotic. You are alive because of his efforts. He has done this in great danger to himself. If he were caught, he'd end like the men outside.

"In revolutions and civil wars, Victor, countries and families are split apart. Ideology and circumstance cause tremendous social upheaval, turning brother against brother. Sometimes the divisions are not mendable, and like Cain and Abel, murder results. There are points of no return, where the errors committed are so grievous, so inhumane and evil, that a truce of humanity is unreachable. This road to perdition, a path of total ruin and loss, is not the only trail available to us. In other times and along other roads, forgiveness prevails, and the fratricide ceases. It is up to each and every man, woman, and child to choose the right path to freedom. I would like to view Samuel's assistance as a sign of hope for our country and people..."

"Do you think Cuba has hope for peace one day?" Asked the boy, understanding the unique situation we were all in. "Do you feel we are on a dark road, full of dangerous impediments and risks to a soulful righteous life, with no exits for salvation; or do you truly believe we can extract goodness and joy for our families and country?"

"The art in me, more than the science, offers me a glimmer of hope," I answered with slight unease. "Creating beauty, whether in color of prose or paint, is like medicine for a physician healer. It provides us with a touch of kind introspection, which political leaders cannot duplicate. Before men can put down arms and stop the killing, they must first enlighten their souls and realize the great gift of life and the human mind. We have the ability to cure diseases, create great works of literature, music, and visual art. One day our science will allow us to travel to the moon, outer planets, and even far away stars. Am I then to believe that we cannot erase the greed and lust for power of just a few sick men?

"Yes, Boy... I feel in my heart that not only can we have peace and joy in our small nation, but also throughout the world today and all the other worlds we may inhabit tomorrow..."

The pass window of our cage door opened. Samuel velázquez' eyes peered through.

"It's time, Jorge... Guevara's men are coming for you. Get prepared..."

I limped up on my good leg and faced the boy on the ground. His eyes opened wide in apprehension...

"I may be in the winter of my life, Victor, but you are not... Neither is Cuba... Do your best to survive, Boy. Cuba will need young men like you to redirect her into the future, a golden future with peace and justice for all..."

"Give him hell, Jorge!" Shouted the boy.

"I am certain to," I said.

When

When majestic mountains crumble to dust and proud stars
sleep...
When our forever turbulent earth's core cools down down
deep,
and lonely sad sunflowers bend away from low light and
weep...

When tall violent blue sea waves stall at highest crest...
When old undefeated champion hearts beat down down
to rest,
and dawn summer suns rise late without zest – in the west...

When passion rose turns from red to black in kind hand...
When timeless laws of motion in the universe no longer
stand,
and no small graces shine on this land...

When the world is confused and you feel used...
When our sacred spirits lay abused and refused,
I will still love you...

Tides and Lady of Sorrows

Great killer tide of tides, war history riptide.
Endless murder torrent flows split sides wide.
Break strong bows and bones and marrows,
many to reign of wood posts and gallows.
Poor, poor lady of sorrows…

Long work day and sleepless night –
Red, blue, and white.
Wash away sin with spite and settle blood fight.
Short weak memory, no wrong or right.
Reckless terror and mass grave trench furrows.
Poor, poor lady of sorrows…

Colors of flag swept beneath tombstone waves,
abandon of spirit virtue and souls without saves.
Soldiers of misfortune ripped in violent raves.
Torn heads and chests, many holes by steel arrows.
Poor, poor lady of sorrows…

No signs of hope, all lines of betrayal.
Surviving eyes only see human fail.
No freedom ship sail in angry wind gale.
Lost dreams and plans for better tomorrows.
Poor, poor lady of sorrows…

To Be Free

To be free...
To leave behind winding endless roads to nowhere,
bottomless pits of the earth,
dark and painful deprivations...

To never consider again questions without answers,
endure empty promises,
or face hopeless dilemmas...

To never see again senseless struggle,
or waste away efforts of spirit
battling evil design...

To never feel lack of faith,
wanting fair and just change -
that never comes,
desiring a bright future that never appears...

To think deeply, to ponder and wonder.
To live, love, and create.
To share beauty.
To be free...

Abstract of Love and War

On white virgin linen canvas – red oil.
Remembrance of bed and battlefield, and of all poetry
said.
Loud amorphous expression of body amor and toil,
vivid mind images of things living and dead.
Thick hot streaks of light and dark sanguine,
without visible forms and shapes figurine…

Eye sees and persists with what it can't forget,
whether be consume of romance love lips in bloom,
or deep debt and high pulse in martial night sweat.
Never too late, never too soon,
reflections come of life destinies met,
moments in real time under fever blood moon…

Cold immersion into scorching crimson cloth,
action potentials dash from retina to brain.
Chemical messengers become pour of liquid froth,
heart eminent domain with gonads insane – to Abel and
Cain.
Inamorato or matador forevermore,
and always fond remember or answer regret for,
in abstract of love and war…

My Beating Heart

Footprints in sand away from me,
vanishing before my eyes with rolling tide...

Orange and blue of sunset,
lonely glow fading to black...

Last whispers of light from gas lantern,
disappearing with blow of wind in dark, dark night...

Scent of perfume,
gone from body but not conscience...

Hold of your love,
unyielding and intense,
burning, freeing and captivating,
intensifying in absence...

My beating heart...

Measure of Life

Measure of life...
Time and quality,
fruit and labor,
friendships and travels...

Rich and poor,
in expense and stories...

Studied and polished,
sophisticated tastes,
or not...

Roads and risks taken,
or avoided...

Ideals and principles believed,
or forgotten.
Virtues lived,
or abandoned...

Fortunes, accomplishments, and trophies.
Reversals and losses...

There is a beginning,
but always also an end.
It must be so...

We thrive, prosper, and flourish.
We endure, persevere, and survive.
We decline, wither, and recede...

At close,
the measure that stands,
the only true value of life –
How much you loved,
how fast you loved,
how long you loved...

I was born when I first laid eyes on you,
and I died after I last did so...
All things in between were you,
and you alone...

I Desire You As

I desire you as…
Shaded grass desires light,
and wilted flower – rain.

I desire you as…
Twilight forest desires songbird,
and cold living stream – warm colored stone.

I desire you as…
Quiet sea and sky desire wind,
and shore – soft white sand.

I desire you as…
Cold winter desires spring,
and black night – day.

I desire you as…
Tired mind desires soul,
and old heart – youth.

I desire you as…
Lonely spirit desires romantic ballad,
and chilled lips – a kiss.

I desire you as...
I desire breath and life,
food and wine,
belief and promise,
dreams.

I desire you as...
You desire me...

How Do I Describe?

How do I describe love that transcends all?
Pictures or words?
Great beauty of prose in all color of light and song I recall.
Sacred majesty of being and glory towards...

In holy fortress of heart, I start.
It is there where memory burns.
Images of you and I like sacred darts,
more and more of me yearns...

In all there was, and all that will be,
in all perfect circles and parallel lines,
in all truth of forms one can see,
desire for more of you raptures like passion vines...

I only hope for no end of lucid dream,
to harmony of minds we feel.
Where all stars shine and moons beam.
Where all hurts heal...

Almighty love, grander than all things.
Gentle and tender secrets perhaps best not told.
Innermost of us that sings,
deepest and most sincere we hold...

Pure love unexplained.
Reality inside of us in never ending bliss.
Not called for, or wished for and attained.
Most fortunate recess of soul, I hope to never miss...

ACT II

Trial

I was taken at rifle point down a long and dark humid cavernous corridor of the old fortress into daylight. Escorted by four militia men, led by a sergeant, I walked past the firing wall while another poor devil was lined up for execution. I could hear the firing squad marching into position behind me as a bayonet poked between my shoulder blades.

"We're waiting for your turn, Poet," laughed the sergeant. "Keep looking forward!" He screamed into my ear.

Men in their cells all around urged me on.

"Sierra, a la Victoria!

"Invencible!

"Cuba libre!"

"Shut your mouths, animals!" Yelled the sergeant.

I still wore the combat stained civilian clothes I had on when taken prisoner a month before. I had a full black beard and disheveled hair, filled with lice from the prison. A wound in my leg, I had kept fresh, trailed drops of blood behind me. I did my best to walk proudly without a limp.

In my life, at times, I had an ability to view the world around me through colored passion glass. Objects and people, even complete scenes, would take on fervent color expressing their temperature of emotion and action. Swaying palms in warm sea breezes could be fluorescent lime green or purple, or a beautiful morning sky – lilac and citrine. A restless ocean could go from white and blue to red and pink. People's faces could reflect their hearts, turning red in violent anger or sensuous passion, green from envy, or blue in sadness. Eyes could be bright and jewel-colored or dead black as coal. Colors were exhibitions of temperatures of being...

A loud discharge of gunfire dispersed a group of seabirds perched on the high limestone wall. They flew away in panic, like they did many times a day. Toward Old Havana they raced. Their flapping wings created a clap sound, similar to the applause of some of the citizenry for Fidel's reign of terror.

I looked up at the sun with my sensitive blue eyes just before being pushed through a door of the Morro Castle by the sea. I was taken through a series of dungy walkways into a small room facing the Caribbean.

I sat by the open window as ordered. A militia guard kept his rifle pointed at my head.

"Don't think about escape, Sierra," said the sergeant before leaving. "It's a long drop onto sharp rocks. Even if you survive, our guns will kill you."

On one wall, there was a large Cuban flag nailed into the stone. The iron nails were twisted out of shape, bent by the beating of a hard hammer. A small rip in the cloth at the center of the white five-pointed star seemed to grow before my very eyes, signaling the division born in our nation at civil war.

Photo portraits of Che Guevara on horseback in the Sierra Maestra mountains, and Fidel Castro marching triumphantly into Havana, were on another wall. Near Castro's image, I could see a solar stain on the old stone wall around where a Christian Cross had once hung.

I bit my tongue in anger and frustration. A small dribble of blood dripped out of my mouth and onto the floor. The guard beside me laughed.

In a short time, my Cuba had changed into an unfamiliar place. I could hardly recognize her. A land with hypnotic attraction, with people so joyous and enlivened by life, had turned into a sick swamp of hateful evil creatures. These 'proud' Cubans had even allowed an unknowing foreigner, Che Guevara, to gain control over their lives. He had become the new 'dictator' of government policy, implementing communist rule with complete impunity.

The room was cold, as my heart. I chose to gaze out the window onto the blue sea.

A young beautiful girl in green army fatigues walked in and placed a cup of steaming hot coffee and a cigar on the table in front of me. She was not stern and rough in appearance; in fact, she seemed like an exotic model ready for a runway in a big city fashion show. She smiled at me, her olive-green eyes matching her uniform.

"El Comandante enjoys all things Cuban," grinned the militia man, still with his rifle point to my temple.

I returned to the sapphire sea... The same sea I had appreciated painting, as in the day of meeting the love of my life. Such different settings, such different countries...

Guevara entered in a hurry and sat across from me. He shuffled some papers in a folder before setting them aside. The Argentinean Marxist stared me down, sipping coffee and lighting his cigar.

"I can't think of a prettier place for a revolution," he laughed with dark brown penetrating eyes. "Rugged nature, rugged women, and a rugged people; I don't ever want to leave."

I drilled back into him with my eyes. Every ounce of energy left in me was focused.

"I just finished meeting with your father, Sierra. He's staying in one of our cells here at the Morro. He's a relatively decent man for a Batistiano. Educated and rich, I wonder why he was at the beaches of Playa Girón?

"I was informed Raul was the oldest fighter in the Yankee-trained combat brigade. A fifty-three year old governor of Las Villas battling against us at the Bay of Pigs. That's incredible...

"Nevertheless, it's not as unbelievable as a poet-painter working behind enemy lines in espionage. Your story, Sierra, is unique. Especially considering you're not a Batistiano...

"How is it the son of the governor of a Cuban province under Batista does not support his regime?

"And fights a liberating army, while still arguing harshly against the past...

"Which side are you on, Sierra?

"A nationalist dictator oppressing his people --- a brutalizing and murderous gangster under control of imperialist Yankees?

"Or the fighters for freedom and liberation of the enslaved people of Cuba?"

Che Guevara motioned for the guard to leave the room. He sat back in his chair and smoked.

"I am an admirer of your poetry and paintings. I believe I've read and seen all of your works. Many of the canvases were at the national museum. Fidel is also an admirer.

"Battling in the mountains of Las Villas, my army and I came across your abandoned hilltop studio. You, of course, were fighting us in those same mountains.

"I confiscated some items to protect them from damage. I hope you don't mind my taking possession of a collection of poems and an interesting red painting titled, 'Abstract of Love and War'. The work hangs over my bed where I fuck my Cuban wife," grinned the delusional Argentinean.

"How are your hands, Sierra?

"I am sorry for the breaking of your fingers after arrival at La Cabaña. The officer in charge disliked your anti-revolutionary paintings of firing squads. He told me they were disgraceful and demeaning of my disciplinary tactics. The fractures of your fingers were beyond my control. Besides, you won't be painting any longer... Unfortunate, but you likely won't have time to see them heal."

Guevara sipped more coffee and smoked.

"Your poems are about the beauties of Cuba, those I have come to know well. They are also about love and war, which I have also come to know well.

"I particularly enjoy three writings... 'SunKissed', 'When', and 'Tides and Lady of Sorrows'.

"There are many more, but those stay in my head like pretty songs."

Guevara slowly recited each one from memory as I stared out the window. I had been tortured enough already.

"As a medical student in Buenos Aires, I'd read Walt Whitman, Pablo Neruda, and John Keats at night in my spare time. Poetry relaxed me immensely. It allowed for a freeing of spirit I couldn't get in the stresses of learning science.

"I also write poetry... It may not be as romantic as yours, but I believe it's fine enough for a revolutionary. I wrote much prose under candlelight in the jungles of Cuba. The written word is a means to clear the mind...

"I greatly respect your work, Sierra. It's loved throughout the world. But I don't believe there'll be a place for it in the new Cuba. Fidel and I agree on this."

The earth tones of the stone room, the grays and browns of the floor and walls, the mossy dark green on creamy coral, the mustard yellows of aging rock, all turned bright red, white, and blue before my eyes – the colors of the flag of country which had now turned on me.

"Your painting is a similar matter," said Guevara, with the Cuban cigar sticking from his mouth. "Many pieces appear somewhat rough against our ideals and philosophies. The works at the museum were moved into storage. Perhaps in a few decades, the regime will forgive your trespasses; or maybe, I will destroy them all. We will see.

"It is sad when an artist loses his countrymen. When the poetry and the art, although remaining beautiful in pure essence, become a source of disagreement with the new establishment. When colors and words rub open sores and create divisions among the great people of Cuba.

"Your abstracts depict injustice and brutality. They are unfair to our regime. They make Fidel and I look like killers, like butchers of Cuba. We cannot allow this misguidance to multiply. It may confuse our people in times of difficulty. The coming years will test all of us reformers gravely. I think the war against America is just beginning. We must keep our people united and focused on extending Cuban communism throughout Latin America and the world. Your art can only get in the way of our goals of anti-imperialism.

"Also, abstract art is not conducive to the development of the moral 'New Man' – a hardworking, selfless and cooperative, obedient, non-materialistic, incorruptible being. Freeing spirits wildly often leads to rebellion, national disunion, and eventual social and financial stratification, wealth concentration and economic inequality. There can be no abstract expressionism in the new State.

"I have had many duties in Cuba... I ran the revolutionary tribunals and instructed the militia. I developed agrarian land reforms. I presently run the national bank, and function as Cuba's leading international diplomat. My great powers in Fidel's revolution allow me to dictate policy... And I assure today, your poetry and paintings will never be recited and seen in this land for years to come."

Guevara wheezed and coughed. He threw the remainder of his cigar out the window.

"I must stop smoking... It only worsens my asthma.

"You are also an asthmatic, Sierra. Your father asked me to be aware of this, as if I'd be caring of the fact...

"You then know the feeling of being unable to take breath, drowning in your own respiratory secretions. It happened to me many times in the jungle, and often without medications to relieve me. I am amazed I didn't suffocate in the wild..."

I had been asthmatic since childhood. It was reactive, like my art. It often shortened my breath; but also, respiratory distress had hardened my nature into a resilient attitude for survival. Each time I was without breath, I'd fight. Easing out of an attack was like being reborn with a second chance. It was part of me, as my skin and senses.

"Well, Sierra... let's get down to business...

"This is your tribunal. It's you and I alone.

"Unlike your father who was taken prisoner as a uniformed combatant on a battlefield, you are a Yankee spy. You were captured behind our lines at Playa Girón during an invasion of the homeland. You were directly responsible for blowing a critical bridge required to send tanks to the beaches. You also killed several of our soldiers while wearing civilian clothes.

"In all other similar circumstances, you would have been killed on the spot. Fate intervened somehow in your case. Perhaps, the destiny of the new Cuba demanded we digest your active presence against the revolution of the people. In longer scrutiny, a decision to eliminate you becomes more solid in the minds of our countrymen. With more time, consideration of your traitorous activity becomes self-evident. I do not want you as a martyr.

"I certainly have made concessions in this special situation. You are a Cuban cultural figure, known dearly to the people. I decided to preside over the trial personally, after a full understanding of your story.

"So here we are, Sierra... Just you and me, and the beautiful Caribbean Sea.

"Speak! And convince me not to kill you..."

In the life of the world come many moments that can decide the future of nations and tribes and individual people - decision points which may lead sometimes to great horrors in the deaths of millions, or to the single death of perhaps a very beloved person. Choices, likewise, can lead to great successes and the extension of quality productive human lives. The intricate fate workings of the world and humanity and personal life may turn on a simple choice made in the backroom of an important government building or scientific laboratory in a significant university. My decision point came in an old stone room of a Cuban castle by the sea, looking out at the most spectacular blue colors I had ever seen...

"I know your story, as you know mine, Guevara...

"As you find my life interesting – as you say – I being a poet-painter in a military struggle, promoting the destruction of an enemy, killing them when opportunities arise; I also find your life interesting, Guevara...

"You studied medicine in your home country, learning the healing arts, perfecting your knowledge in the workings of the human body and disease. You immersed yourself in the details of human anatomy and physiology, pharmacology, and surgery. The full intent of your investment was to cure people of illness, improving their lives; and in many successful instances, giving second chances to live. You became a man of life sciences.

"I too learned science. I studied high level mathematics and physics, taking in great knowledge on the physical workings of the universe.

"There was, however, a singular important difference in our formal educations... My training was in physical science.

It was numerical and completely objective. It afforded little opportunity for studying human nature.

"You, on the other hand, learned much about human nature on a daily basis. Caring for the gravely ill and dying, you held many hands in their last moments. You must have realized even more intimately than I in my poems and paintings, the truest values of human life – our needs for affection and love, our duties to family and the care of the young, our wishes to be truly good in this world...

"There must not be any more significant impact than feeling with your fingertips the last heartbeat of a mother or child, and know inside your own heart that no more wishes for truth and humanity can be fulfilled. It must leave in you a permanent reminder of the frailty and fragility of life, and the final innate desires of a person to have done good in their lives.

"There will be some who argue in history that it was this very experience of yours which led you to choose a life of international rebellion and Marxist existence. The neglect and abuse of the impoverished, the uneducated peasant classes, the indigenous indians of Latin America and Africans may have directed you to blame North American capitalism and imperialism. That somehow white man's greed and lust for wealth and power led to slavery and the abuse of poor underclasses. That seeing their misery and death up close enraged you to armed struggle against the oppressors.

"I, on the other hand, think the medical experience should have enlightened you to a life of intelligent and humane design. While healing hundreds of thousands in a medical lifetime, you could have also promoted deep discussion of all the unfair human issues inflicted on society.

You could have had a significant peaceful social influence on a grand scale if you had wished; certainly much grander than my words of prose or works on canvas, I believe...

"Your love of poetry and literature could have influenced you on paper as well. Instead of writing books on guerrilla warfare, you may have written of good deeds, love, and the infinite beauties of being alive in this wonderful physical universe. Instead of writing treatises on Marxism and Cuban communism, you perhaps would have defined better the human potential of man's better natures. You had an opportunity like no other, one which most people would have mortgaged their lives for...

"All human activity is prompted by desire. Some desires are for basic essentials of life, like water and food, shelter, and procreation. But much more significant than these is the desire for acquisition and power. The emotions involved with human vanity and rivalry have much to do with the desire for absolute power.

"It is innate in all of us that we wish for alimentation and protection of a roof, and for sex. I believe every man, woman, and child on Earth have and will have these desire needs throughout their lifetimes. The act of hoarding, whether it be of food or money, gives our minds a sense of protection. Building great human capital wealth is simply an exaggerated form of this biological drive for permanent sustenance. The American and Western capital structure is born from this innate biological drive. Regardless of communism in the Soviet Union and China, and many other third world countries, Marxist ideology will eventually succumb naturally to human nature.

"While vanity can be satisfied rather easily with glory, like that of a film star or artist, desire for power is not. The acquisition of power only begets the continuous fight for more power. The final goal is total power and omnipotence. Tyranny is the end result of lust for power in energetic men.

"Some political ideologies leave no room for personal liberty and freedoms. Communism eliminates the individual spiritually, and absorbs its last vestiges into the concept of State. The lack of individual creative thinking creates mental midgets and slaves of the controlled system, thereby increasing the power of the more energetic men leaders at the top of the communist hierarchy. Communism depends on tyrannical control of the people. They must be forced to believe and worship the cult images directing them.

"The human animal must also have excitement. In ancient prehistoric times, and in today's times, the excitement of the hunt is primordial. Modern sports and politics provide the masses with the circus needed to excite them. Rivalry is essential to this concept. In sports, teams may be ardent rivals; but in political ideological systems, rivalry must be turned fanatically towards an enemy. The classic example today is the dangerous rivalry between capitalism and communism. And while capitalism exists in democratic nations, where legislative bodies and courts control the masses, communist states depend on the oppressive whims of political tyrants and their close confidential protectors.

"If a dictator – regardless of whether he be nationalist like Hitler or communist like Stalin - decides to direct his loyal mobs toward a political enemy, there is no congress or court to stop him. In tyrannical systems, the mob is used like a knife to a personal enemy's throat.

"In Cuba, we had a nationalist despot wielding the knife before the revolution; now, we have Fidel and yourself. The mob ruled in both cases. As times pass and get harder economically, the mob will require more and stronger doses of opium excitement. Condemnations will spread wide and far to wars of ideology. You and Fidel will soon require spreading your revolution to Central and South America, and even to Africa and Asia. Opium will become the arsenic of the Cuban people.

"You will instill in our people great fear and hatred of the enemy, because in doing so you will empower yourselves for providing needed security. The people will feel 'safe' with your control of the security apparatus, although it will be inhumanely used against the very people requesting it. You will be perceived as altruistic, rather than protective of your own power. It is a giant masquerade.

"In a system as this, every Cuban must abdicate human dignity, reason, and conscience. We must all assume a position of subservience to those in power, allowing their ambitions and covetous desires. Justice and humanity do not exist.

"Each man must decide for himself what is just and reasonable, what is patriotic... The cult of image and control in Cuba is inexcusable. We are a small island in the Caribbean, in a giant Earth, in an infinite universe. The only cult image should be a god of creation, even if it may exist only in the mind. We humans are too small to merit adoration.

"We have become a country of immorality, with a general lack of nobility and righteous order. We have overthrown a despot and replaced him with a tyrant. What people we are...

"We are forced to work for the 'well-being' of the State. With no pay, there is no real work in time. Slowly the culture will die without money, without literature, without visual art, without philosophy.

"You rely on the failings of the Latin American martyr culture, the lost citizen always searching like an orphan waif for fatherly guidance. It is sickening to watch your pathetic saintly approach to murder and imposition of failed economic and political thinking.

"You are a Marxist puritanical zealot, the windmill chasing dreamer of communism. You are paradoxical, with multiple contradictory personalities and ways of conduct.

"I once painted an abstract Christ, dead from the cross, surrounded by the lamentations of those who loved him. It was a symbolic gesture toward a kind loving man image who gave all for humanity. It was a sacrificial image, pure to its core in gesture... Somehow, I believe you have Christ aspirations of the mind, although you don't believe in a god. Like my picture, you will end dead, as we all will, but I doubt history will truly absolve you.

"Your thoughts on a utopian existence is a pipe-dream. The strict absolutism will not last the test of time. Human nature exists even more so in the poorest and hungriest of us. The mob will eventually turn on you, as it always has in revolution.

"I understand the perfect ideal for humanity. I also understand it doesn't exist. That is the difference between you and I. You are unwilling to accept man's moral deficiencies. You try to annihilate them as a painter destroys a perceived failing on his canvas. You simply wash it away from history, pretending the problem has been eliminated.

"The human brain is not made equally. People have different innate senses of responsibility and work ethic. Some will work harder, some will be more curious and perfection oriented, others less so. But in not allowing and rewarding personal creativity and freedom of choice and expression, you will lead the populace into a dark and painful abyss of non-work and absenteeism. The nationalization of banks, industries and businesses, the confiscation of private lands and possessions, all will lead to a nation of gangsterism and moral depravity.

"You believe in Marxist social science, as I believe in Newtonian physics and Darwinian biology. I agree with you that Man should not be a slave of his social environment; that he should dictate his own destiny. But you fail to realize the most basic tenet of human achievement – the innate desire to create and express oneself in things productive. Without freedom to think and wonder and ponder the problems of humanity, there will be no humanity.

"Your strange and psychotic detachment from violence, especially for a man trained in the healing arts, is incomprehensible. The ruthlessness and brutality of your actions, the shooting of all deemed traitorous to the revolution without legal due process, the turning over of justice to the excited and unruly mobs of Cuba is unforgiveable. Regardless of the injustices of the previous regime, there is no honor in further and even more inhumane injustice. This is not a path for the passions of Cuba.

"You have been Castro's sage and henchman; and thus, I place most blame on you. If you want truly an example of righteous virtue, of honor, of noble cause, this product we have now of Cuba is an utter failure. History will judge you so...

"You may say you accepted the role of guerrilla fighter by accident, that you began as the physician for the revolutionaries; but I know better. Your envy and rage against the economic and military might of the United States, their scientific excellence, and their struggles against the immoralities of the world - required you to take up arms. It is a personal vendetta you have as a communist to defeat and vanquish the world capitalism of America. Cuba was simply a convenient start for you on the revolutionary trail. The Cuban people are to be used like tools in this struggle.

"Your idea of a united Hispanic America, borderless, and in constant struggle against the United States is a fool's play. Our giant to the north will not let you live long enough to even begin.

"Maybe your Irish ancestry has gotten the best of you, locking you in an eternal rebel mood. But I suggest you reconsider the plight of Cuba. Perhaps you should thank Kennedy for his weak knees at Playa Girón, giving you another chance for peaceful reform. Time may be running out, Guevara…

"Instead of reading Neruda, Keats, and Whitman, I believe you should concentrate on Freud and Nietzsche. Read about the interpretation of dreams, and the stark ugly truths of Man and mortality."

Che Guevara stayed motionless in his chair for a long while. His eyes locked into mine. Neither of us blinked.

He removed his beret and placed it softly on the table. He passed his hand through his hair, and then beard. The silence continued…

"Sergeant at arms!" Guevara screamed.

The militia soldiers reentered the room with their guns pointed.

"Return this pathetic worthless traitor to his cell. But first, beat him to a blind and bloody pulp with your fists. Break every one of his fingers again. Take your time outside in the corridor. I wish to relish in his yelp."

Only the Good

Always for you, I wished only the good –
Golden shield and sword of truth and noble cause.
Avoiding barren paths, devoid, dark, and rude;
awaiting warm fair light, we bow and pause.

In past nocturnal stumbles I wandered across
numbing freeze of polar winter and black day,
with endless dry godless fire of desert loss.
Of these ruins, I want none for you I say.

Roads winding and twisting farther and farther away from
me,
disappearing from misty sight but not heart and mind.
The soft smile and tiny hands and feet I still see,
tho missing the touch, the laugh, and gentle natures that
bind.

Great temples of wisdom and learning will call,
child grow with Olympian eternal flower, song, and food.
Time to empower kind body and spirit, and stand tall –
For you, I wished only the good…

Growing Old with You

Hoped to see the day,
our hair white and gray,
hearts tired but strong,
memories joyous and long.

Hoped to see the day,
my hand undying in your hand,
living love in our land.

Hoped to see the day,
my lips trembling to kiss your,
our bodies aching and sore.

Hoped to see the day,
our children happy and free,
my soul forever married to thee.

Perhaps I prayed too much,
wishing always for your touch.

Hoped to see the day,
as you beside me lay...

Once

Once there was a time,
youth and beauty sublime.
Nature's splendor all around,
dream and sound faith found.

Time and we passed,
not all good things last.
Thoughts of tomorrow fade,
loss of promises made.

Now without you – nothing,
no magnificence of being.
Yet, once I could say,
life and love ruled the day.

Deathstar

Deathstar, near and far...
Where energies go, and all life springs,
opening Time and Space ajar,
from atom burst, glory sings.

Jets of light into vast black,
infinite speed without sound.
Building new worlds and zodiac,
fresh suns and planets bound.

Carbon to carbon,
fresh DNA to ash,
cycles of heaven garden,
repeat eternal flash to flash.

Man's story on Earth,
but split second in God's song.
Live each birth with worth,
for we don't have much long.

Do good deed, not bad,
help young aspiring fawn.
To small humanity add,
before chance is gone.

Make great, create, and love,
joy to play guitar in fortress alcazar.
Push away unjust and unworthy of,
before return voyage – Deathstar...

Almighty Father

Almighty Father…
Hear my simple prayer in whisper…
I deliver myself to you.
My failings as true fighter and resistor,
thru and thru now only residue…

I have done my sure best,
serving family and country…
Weak I am without rest,
divided from whole – no entity…

Mortal hope and faith vanished,
only traces of corporeal life remain.
Body flesh torn and savaged,
immortal spirit tho – without chain.

Guard my wife and sweet child,
spare much hurt and deep sorrow.
Leave all doubts in relief and reconciled,
providing calm space for gentle tomorrow.

Take my soul at will – in peace and love,
as you Almighty – and only you – can.
I wish the same for all humane on earth and above,
but save infernal fire for elements enemy of Man…

Shining Path

Hidden glory hath along the shining path...
Lit bright by dawn's inspiring rising sun,
road of white grim stone to the end.
Flanked by evil torment and injustice done,
to my commanded bodily death – they send.

Men frenzied by dark abrupt undeserved power,
with hatred for all things good and pure.
Behind greed, sinister deed, and lust they flower,
torture and murderous appetite without cure.

Cold fancy and insanity rule the mob,
betrayal of all soulful peace I love.
Many good innocent lives they rob,
under the guise of the calm white dove.

In heart I carry sharp arrows of art and poetry,
adoration of wife, child, and country.
Those I painted and wrote verse about,
now destroy me without regret or doubt.

We have lost all sense and humanity,
great ideals and virtues thrown to wrath.
My gravity in their sharp-tongued profanity,
no amnesty hath along the shining path...

By Light of the Moon, Beauty Appears

Dark dark night, white white moon...
Angel round face marked by holes, like our souls...
Bright light through purple black high noon...
Grand power force to illuminate from inside your poles...

Shine strong past iron prison gate on old stone,
show me the way...
Allow me, and me alone, to work work away,
to finish my gift today...

Guide my broken hand to fate,
I pray it's not too late...
Permit me one last glory desire,
to show my love in red fire...

Her special being appears,
slowly in time...
Her look locks and sears,
like poetry in rhyme...

Eyes swallow whole,
lips full and smooth...
Take my bones to toll,
quiet energies soothe...

Paint with blood and soil,
no pastel oil...
Scratch and tear at rock, I dare,
I must show her fair...

Beauty appears by light of the moon,
strokes and shades just right...
Quick I toil with sharp spoon, my end will come soon,
regardless of mind and might...

Thank you, Lord, for the chance to show –
a trial of art expression in advance, I know...
I leave a human trace of long and true love,
for all to see – for your eyes, and mine, from above...

Fuego

Dark and damp in my cage...
Flesh and bone have tired.
Little of me remains.
I am at end of my physical voyage.
Query and doubt and wishful design have gone.
You provide the only tender light.

I love you...
Tresses of ebony hair,
almond orbs radiant and profound,
soft curves of face and lips - inviting.
Smooth but firm shoulders and arms,
the delicate hands,
and graces of your dance.
Sensuous breasts, hips, thighs, and naked feet.
I have indulged in you...

Your gaze, your look,
the brightness and calor of your eyes,
and wide smile.
The tilt of your head,
the resonance of your beating heart on my palm,
the mounds and valleys and rivers of fertile body.
I have indulged in you...

At center of all – your soul.
Quiet ways, loving and kind.

Gentle you are.
I have indulged in you...

I love you in every way – in all ways,
in all color and shade,
in all light,
in all aromas and touch,
in all time and dimension...

We are ghosts now,
divided by space and future,
beaten down by circumstance,
betrayed by unlucky misdirection,
disposed of as waste...

Our energies disregarded by misfortune,
displaced by others uncaring.
Spirits despaired in a maelstrom of inhumanity...

Alas, treacherous blue cavernous currents run deep,
angry winds blow violent,
nature's powers strike like whips.
A great sorrow...

Yet, our love burns – hot.
Like white fire,
stronger than the storm,
beyond all cosmic force,
past all luminant glow,
into vast black eternal ether it rages,
infinite...

ACT III

Last Hours

"Chiquillo," said Samuel Velázquez in a low voice... "Chiquillo," he repeated through the small barred door window.

"Please answer me, Jorge," he pleaded in a whisper.

It had rained overnight. The wet stone floor under full moonlight had been my bed for the past hour. My body felt like an old bag of broken bones -- my feet and hands crushed, mouth busted with teeth missing, chest with ribs aching, and a low constant ring in my ears.

Guevara's men had done their duty for the Comandante, beating me down enough to weaken but not kill. Che wanted the final process to be formal, and carried out ceremoniously. He needed to show the people what wrong words and pictures could do.

The boy beside me nudged my side, and I winced... He pointed with his finger to the door.

I slowly lifted my body and moved to see Velázquez. Our breaths came close.

"I am sorry, Chiquillo... We know not what we do... Please forgive me," cried the guard.

"It is beyond time for forgiveness, Samuel. At least for now... Perhaps, it will be for another generation of Cubans to forgive. Although only God can absolve all our sins," I sounded with a mouth full of blood.

"Have you finished her?" Samuel asked.

"I did..."

Samuel lowered his head in the darkness and sobbed quietly.

"Good," he said in a low but strong voice. "It is for all of us, Jorge... For all of Cuba."

I opened my tired mind and saw her in all her glory. Her beauty so distinct and unique it would water eyes. She was my treasure.

"How am I here, Chiquillo?" Samuel asked with all the regrets in the world. "How is it I fell for all the lies and betrayals, accepting the abuses of our people, and watching while they destroy a culture? Why, Jorge?"

"Only you know, Samuel... They will be questions maybe not even lifetimes could answer... You fell with all the others into the mob. Now it will be up to you to disentangle from the evil web, and place the future of Cuba in your cleared eyes."

"I don't know if I have that strength, Chiquillo..."

"Then, if you and all the others show no respect for humanity, what is the future of our nation to be?

"Will our people become worthless and ignorant tools for egomaniacs and gangsters?

"Will Cuba be shaped into a terrorist nation, promoting sinister acts around the world?

"Do we as a people not care to be ruled by animals from the zoo?

"To be spied on, watched and listened for every doing and word considered against the sacred revolution of confused men?

"Is that the destiny of an intelligent and passionate people?

"No, Samuel... I believe it impossible chaos should rule forever... Eventually, clear minds prevail... And a sinking ship will be saved."

"How is it, Chiquillo, that even as a boy you had golden reason? Clear thoughts to decide clear paths? I saw it in your earliest paintings of the mountains, rivers, and sea. You could capture the love even in a blade of grass..."

I could sense all the regrets in Velázquez --- confused in an abused life. I could also feel the love in him, for me and our country. Many hundreds of years of colonial rule by despotic Spanish, many failed rebellions and small wars for independence, had created a passionate tormented people prone to abrupt decision and miscalculation.

Weeping again, Samuel said, "At sunrise, they will execute you by firing squad... Guevara placed a bloody post for you by the Morro and sea. He wants your father to hear the shots of your death; and also, he desires you to view the sea you love so much for a last time. He is a sick sadistic man of contradiction."

I thought of my father... He had governed a country province under Batista's government, sometimes in disagreement with the policies from Havana. I had argued with him many times about the injustices of a nationalist dictatorship. His aggressive anti-communist position had forced him to accept the lesser of evils, he thought.

I remembered painting as a child a portrait of him and I on the farm, standing together side by side. My father had been fond of it, and I had caught him many times viewing the work in the evenings alone.

I knew my father would miss me dearly if he lived, as I had missed him nearly all my life. We both had regrets also.

"Would you like me to speak with your father?" Gently asked Samuel.

"Yes," I answered softly, still in my own remembrances. "Tell him, I've always done all I could for our country and people, as I know he did. Tell him, I'm sorry for the sad ending, and that I've always loved him like the sea loves the sky."

"And your wife and child in Miami?" Wept Samuel.

"If one day you are able, let them know how much I adored them. That they were always in my thoughts and dreams, in every letter of every poem and every flash of brush on every canvas I painted. Tell my wife she was the light of my soul and the beat of my heart.

"Hold my young Olivia's hand, and tell her about me, and how I always wished for her happiness and love prosperity. Let her know how much I loved and cherished her. Tell her, that not even eternity will stamp out the fire of love I had for her."

"I will be with you till the end, Jorge; all of Cuba will be."

Samuel passed his fingers through the bars and across my beaten face. He pulled my ear in a tender way, like he had done many times in my youth to stress a point.

"You are a great man, Chiquillo... The fineness of your poetry and art cannot match the fineness of your truth."

"They are one and the same," I answered.

Samuel Velázquez retired slowly into the pitch blackness of the prison stone, like a ghost in a dream.

I returned to the boy's side. He had been awake, listening to our realities.

"It is almost dawn, Jorge," he said with great fear and sadness in his voice. "Is there no hope left?"

"There is no hope for me, Boy... But you are better from your wound, and you are a uniformed soldier of the resistance. Fidel will likely spare your life, if he has a single bone of dignity remaining. America will become more involved, and at least make attempts to right her wrongs. I have faith you and many others will live. Stay strong and survive this ordeal. Cuba needs her boys courageous for the long struggle to come.

"Sleep now... We will say our goodbyes in the light of the sun," I urged the boy.

Victor, exhausted to sleepiness, drifted off into his own dreams... I also did, turning to gaze at my creation... In an internal melody hymn of thought, my mind went into a soliloquy of love, loss, desire and longing for my wife, child, country, and world...

Will death be forever dream?
And was life with you not so?
In Space vacuum split in seam
Reality and abstract mix and go

In mystic tunnel Time
With no start or end

Eternal fall or climb
With no stop or bend

To begin or finish
I do not know
To relive or diminish
At a high or low

Will you be with me?
Song of shooting comet flight
I alone, or together we
Cold tears, or stars delight

Bodies apart, but spirits no
Entwined rapturous snakes
In silent mind and flow
Bliss ever-last, heartbreaks

By light of the moon
I lay in needy want
Aspiring to touch soon
Heaven piedmont

Bones broken
Tattered dreams
Words unspoken
Alone under moonbeams

Wishing to see and feel
Your quiet beauty form
You my angel soul ideal
Keep my heart warm

I have worked till end
With crushed finger and spoon
In sacred soil and blood blend
A life tempest typhoon

Every curve and line
Lips, regal nose, and eyes
Every soulful sign
Before my last sunrise

In Elysian poetic art
Love fulfilled and lack
Like flower and poison dart
To paradise and back

To put one's insides
On ancient coral stone
Without secular guides
Only on holy time loan

To depict final effort
Exhibit the world a lesson
Paint a picture of hurt
And also love possession

Under torture and duress
Work without stop
Attain a level purest
Expend last teardrop

At finish, as at the start
I kneel in prayer and stare

And feel ripped apart
Remembering fine girl so rare

Like hanging over burning fire
Fingertips losing grip
Moment so bleak and dire
No time, no bargain chip

Living out every second
Aware of every heart-beat
Hear your voice beckon
Anthem tender and sweet

You call for me to sail
And wait for you out there
Seal goodbye with kiss inhale
I smile under lunar glare

I would have wished
To hold you in my arms
Never to love missed
Exist in all your charms

Alas, I will now in freedom go
With you in me, tracks our own
Take me where Cuban winds blow
Where love clears paths unknown...

Night went to day... The light of the mighty Cuban sun rose above the ocean horizon. The smell of the robust sea was in my cage. My Lady sparkled out of stone and into me, like a strong wind into my lungs. I sensed her power in me, as iron in a sword...

The march of soldiers came to me. Time had arrived…

"Sierra, up with you!" Screamed the officer, followed behind by three militia men. "It is time, Poet, to meet your maker, and pay your bill to Fidel."

Jorge Sierra stood on his own, as a soldier stuck a rifle butt into his belly and another slapped his face.

The officer in charge saw the work on the wall. He went into a rage of words.

"Go get the Comandante! He must see this for himself!" He ordered one of the troops.

"In our new Cuba, there is adoration of only the State and Fidel!" Yelled the officer.

"Begin the walk to hell, Sierra!"

Without limp, the patriot walked strongly out the hall to open light. He was barefoot, and bleeding from many body wounds. Shirtless, his pants were stripped in a thousand pieces. As he passed Samuel Velázquez, Sierra whispered thanks for helping keep the boy alive. The guard had done a noble service in his great ignoble disservice.

The prisoners of La Cabaña were silent, like holding a Divine Mass for the dead. They stood at their bars, staring out.

The poet-painter walked a long gauntlet of soldiers towards the Morro. Some spat, others kicked and shoved their weapons into him.

"Hijo de puta!… Cabrón!" They screamed.

A prisoner began singing the Cuban national anthem. He was joined by many others.

Sierra was taken to a wooden post on a green grassy promontory by the Morro Castle, facing the blue sea. A warm spring Caribbean wind blew over him, watering his eyes. He could still hear the men singing their anthem.

Che Guevara entered Sierra's cell to view the composition on the wall.

"What is this?" He asked a soldier in anger.

"His Lady," answered the militia man.

"Cuba!" Said the injured boy in loud and proud voice, before having his skull smashed.

"Wash it away!" Yelled Guevara...

Eight riflemen presented themselves in front of Sierra. They stood at attention, waiting for their order.

"Do you have any last wishes, Poet?" Asked the officer, before tying Jorge Sierra to the post.

The patriot slowly looked at the sea and took a deep breath. He then bent down and placed his hands into Cuba's rich fertile soil. He softly smeared the dark earth on his chest, and face around his blue eyes - framing them in a saintly picture of devotion.

The firing squad all turned their faces away in deep shame. Samuel Velázquez from a distance cried silent tears.

Now secured around the wooden pillar, Jorge Sierra looked toward the rising sun and the light that had marked his great works of art, and declared in a powerful voice, "My Cuba, my Wife, my Olivia... I pray the sun never sets on the precious loves of my life. I hold faith God will protect them as dearly as I have."

The communist officer raised his hand in the air and fiercely brought it down, "FUEGO! Fuego! fuego!"

Epilogue

Daybreak

Daybreak mercy, pacify tender people's plight
Ignite inner might infinite to soulful ease
Yellow beams of love light unite in foresight
Tame sweet - inner dictator - without appease

Black sea, purple sky – from restless slumber awaken
Sun of suns rise with spirit glowing golden streams
Reveal new roads for lost land forsaken
Burn demonic schemes, illuminate noble dreams

Infuse God's wisdom for proper equal free will
Set back those evil, who destroy and maim
Give skill to channel empathy and compassion still
Remind stubborn enemy of old and future same

Make way for new day of thought composition
Enlighten, and rid old prejudice argument
Reason to settle score without inquisition
Urge cultural mends with mutual acknowledgement

Paint pictures and write words of freedom birthright
Vanish abuse of power and murder of innocent life

Like white knight of letters, kind poetry recite
Be better humankind than past, avoid further strife

Daybreak mercy, break day with powered inspiration
No more time to waste, after all past wasted time
Abstain from violent hatred and vengeful retribution
Build a nation without war – in eternal peace sublime...

Acknowledgements

I would like to thank Ramón Cernuda for his friendship and long hours of instruction and enlightenment on the history of Cuba and her art. In order to write the poetry and narrative of FUEGO, I first needed to understand the minds of creative artists throughout Cuba's odyssey. Ramón, with a long tradition of promotion of the visual arts as a primary form of freedom expression, was essential to my understanding. I have cherished his time spent with me in a long two-year discovery odyssey of my own. Reaching an ultimate epiphany, it allowed for my furious writing of FUEGO in six weeks.

I am also deeply appreciative of Ramón's wife, Nercys - and son, Sergio, and his wife, Luisa – all of them friends. With Ramón, they have developed the finest gallery of art in the world for Cuban creations – Cernuda Arte of Coral Gables, Florida. I have seen many beautiful wonders, spanning centuries, at their devoted gallery. My wife, Alina, and I have great affection for the Cernuda family.

As in all my prior books, love for my family has been at the core of my creation. My parents, brother and sister, as well as grandparents and extended family, are all in my heart always.

My children – Julio, Ali, Michael, and Marcus – are the source of my energy. I love them more than life.

Alina, my wife and best friend, my love soulmate, my everything... You are FUEGO, and all other fine passionate things of mind... I love you.

www.ingramcontent.com/pod-product-compliance
Lightning Source LLC
Chambersburg PA
CBHW021129130626
46554CB00002B/924